THE VAMPIRES
NEXT DOOR

SIGI COHEN   PATRICK CORRIGAN

The mystery began when a girl known as Lee
saw dozens of bats, upside down in a tree.

The tree stood alongside a house down the lane
belonging to Horace, Drusilla and Shane.

"Our neighbours are vampires!"
said Lee to her dad

but he gave her a look
like he thought she was mad!

The first one to vanish
was Edie Caruthers;
The next disappearance -
The Beverley brothers.

Detectives arrived asking
lots of strange questions,
and some of the neighbours
had crazy suggestions...

"The Boogieman got them!"
cried Fergal McNairy,
wriggling his fingers and trying to look scary.

The very next evening the truth became clear
when Lee felt a bite just below her left ear.

She slapped her neck hard,
heard an "ouch" sort of sound
and Horace, her neighbour,
fell flat on the ground!

He started to screech till his face became blue:
"How dare you attack me - I'm stronger than you!

You'll be the next human that I dine upon.
Soon all of the kids on this street will be GONE!"

Well, after her neighbour's bad-tempered display,
he sprouted some wings and he fluttered away...

The very next morning - Lee rode to the deli

and bought lots of garlic bread,
fresh-baked and smelly.

She peddled back home and started to eat,
and she ate 'til her breath
smelt much worse than her feet.

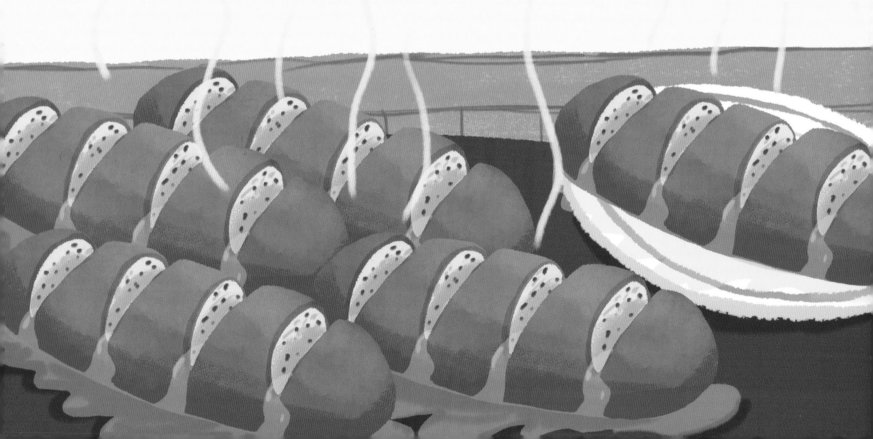

At sunset she crept towards Horace's house

and peered through the keyhole, as still as a mouse.

From down in the cellar she heard a weird sound –

Some hideous noises from under the ground.

She went down a stairway, opened a door,
and was shocked and amazed at the sight that she saw.

The cellar was teeming with dozens of bats
with sharp, pointy teeth and pink, party hats.

Horace was singing a rock 'n' roll song,
and Shane, his great grandpa, was howling along.

Drusilla was sipping what looked like red tea,
and they froze on the spot when they recognised Lee.

The vampires were startled and taken aback.
In spine-chilling voices, they shouted: "Attack!"
They turned into bats as big as Lee's arm,
and circled her head as she tried to stay calm.

buurrpp

Screeching and flapping, they flew at her face,
but Lee stood her ground with great courage and grace.
A bat tried to bite her - she heard it go "slurp",
so she let off a powerful garlicky burp...

Twenty-three bats fell, stunned, to the floor,
so she burped once again and she dropped twenty more.
The bats couldn't handle her garlicky smell,
as she burped and she burped 'til the final bat fell.

buurrpp

If you think, for a bat, that's as bad as it gets -
a ranger arrived with some very strong nets.

And now there's a total of seventy-two
Vampire Bats on display at the zoo.

And trapped in a cage where they'll always remain

are Horace, Drusilla and great-grandpa Shane.

Sigi Cohen

Sigi Cohen was raised in South Africa and lives in Perth, Western Australia. Aside from writing for kids, Sigi works as a lawyer which he says greatly alleviates the stresses of writing children's picture books!

He is the author of the darkly funny 'My Dead Bunny', 'Filthy Fergal', 'There's Something Weird About Lena' and 'Zombie Schoolteachers'.

Sigi writes quirky stories that both children and adults enjoy reading aloud. He entertains young readers through humorous, appealing (sometimes appalling) over-the-top tales that come alive with illustrations.

Patrick Corrigan

Patrick Corrigan was born on a crisp, cold December day in a small, cloudy town in Cheshire, England. With a passion for precision as a child, he grew up patiently drawing and designing arts and crafts.

This took him to study ceramics at University, train as an art teacher and eventually become an Art Director at a busy design studio where he worked for nearly 10 years. Whilst there he honed his skills working on well over 500 educational and picture books for children as well as animations and branding.

Patrick specialises in illustrating picture books for younger readers and draws best when listening to podcasts or dusty old records and drinking gallons of green tea

Larrikin House
142-144 Frankston Dandenong Rd, Dandenong South Victoria 3175 Australia
www.larrikinhouse.com

First Published in Australia by Larrikin House 2021 (larrikinhouse.com)

Written by: Sigi Cohen
Illustrated by: Patrick Corrigan
Cover Designed by: Mary Anastasiou
Design & Artwork by: Mary Anastasiou (imaginecreative.com.au)

A CIP catalogue record for this book is available from the National Library of Australia. http://catalogue.nla.gov.au

ISBN: 9781922503084 (Hardback)
ISBN: 9781922503091 (Paperback)
ISBN: 9781922503107 (Big Book)

FORESTFRIENDLY
This book is printed on paper sourced from sustainable forests

NATIONAL LIBRARY OF AUSTRALIA

A catalogue record for this book is available from the National Library of Australia